This book belongs to

Written by Rosie Greening.
Illustrated by James Dillon.

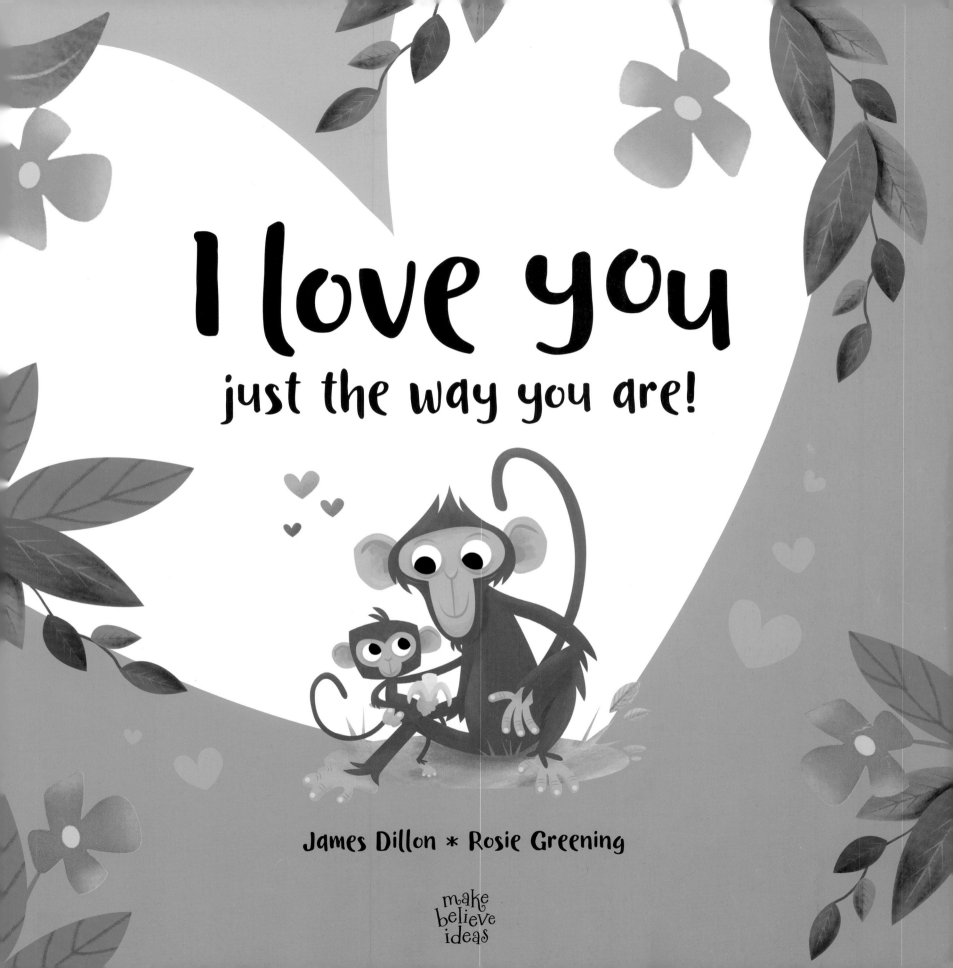

I love you
just the way you are!

James Dillon * Rosie Greening

make
believe
ideas

Each morning, when I wake you up, you're **grumpy** as can be.

But you're my dreamy dozer, and that's **alright** with me.

When you're feeling **nervous**, you sometimes try to **hide**.

But **I love you**, timid **tortoise**, and I'm **always** by your side.

Even though you're **tiny**, you're the **bravest** mouse I know.

I love you, little **lionheart** –
it's great to **watch** you **grow**.

You always make
a lot of MESS
each time you
eat and play.

Although you are a mucky **pup,**
I love you anyway.

You like to **trumpet** loudly, and **stomp** and **stamp** all day.

You're a noisy **elephant,**
but **I love you** that way.

You **scramble** and you **SCURRY.** You **clamber** and you **climb.**

You're my cheeky **monkey** and **I love you** all the time.

Whenever we go **SWIMMING**, you're the splashiest by far.

You're my happy **hippo**
and **I love** how fun you are.

Sometimes you **don't** want a **wash,**
and give a giant **ROAR.**

Even when you're **stubborn,** every day **I love you** more.

When you're in a **prickly** mood,
you **curl** up in a ball.

But you're my spiky **hedgehog** and **I love you** most of all.

Sometimes you **jump** happily

and **never** want to stop.

You're a fidget, little **frog,**
but **I love** every hop.

Whether you're red and **angry**,

or feeling **down** and **blue**,

I see all your **true colours,**
and the **beauty** inside you.

So remember, in the universe, you are **MY brightest star.**

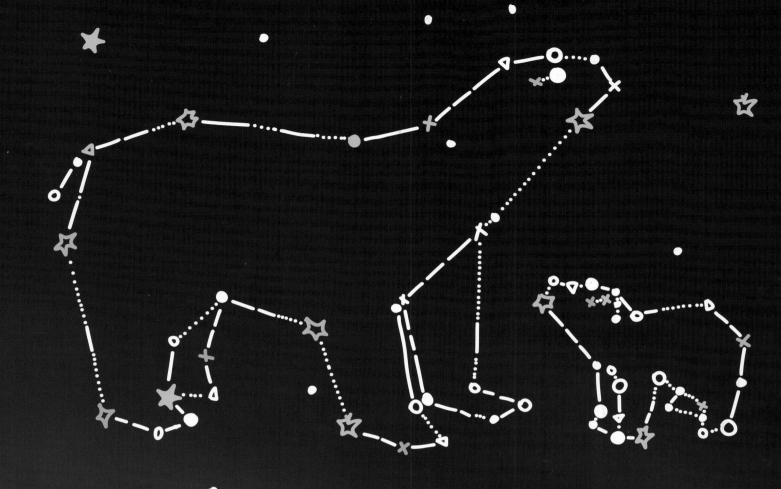

And **no matter what** you say or do,
I love you as you are!

The End